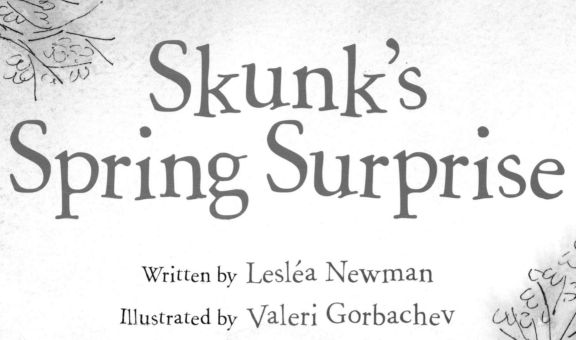

Skunk's
Spring Surprise

Written by Lesléa Newman

Illustrated by Valeri Gorbachev

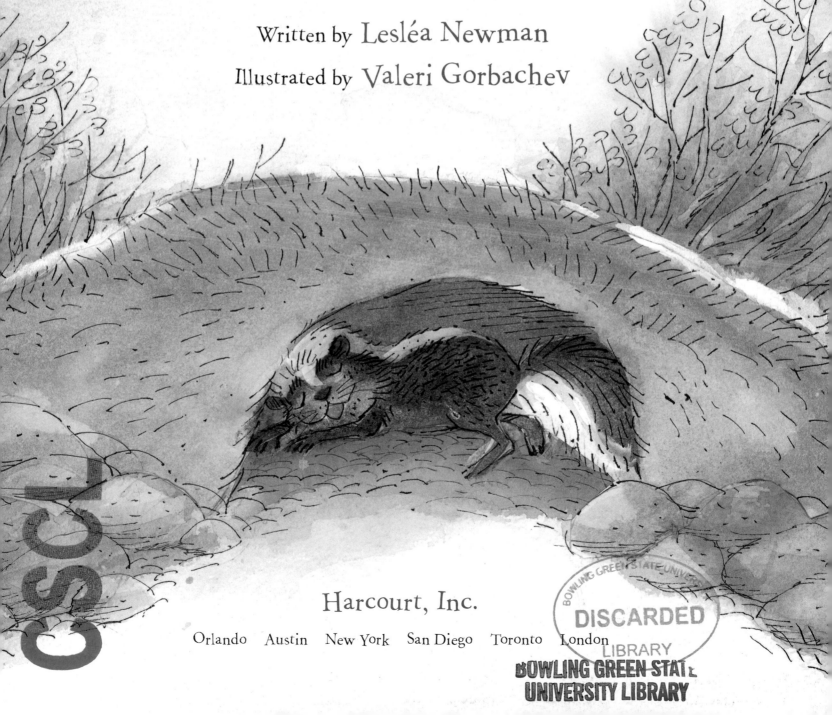

Harcourt, Inc.

Orlando   Austin   New York   San Diego   Toronto   London

Library of Congress Cataloging-in-Publication Data
Newman, Lesléa.
Skunk's spring surprise/written by Lesléa Newman; illustrated by Valeri Gorbachev.
p.   cm.
Summary: After waking from her winter nap, Skunk worries that her friends have forgotten her, but it turns out they have planned a spring surprise.
[1. Skunks—Fiction.   2. Forest animals—Fiction.   3. Talent shows—Fiction.   4. Stories in rhyme.]
I. Gorbachev, Valeri, ill.   II. Title.
PZ8.3.N4655Sku   2007
[E]—dc22   2005004383
ISBN-13: 978-0-15-205683-4   ISBN-10: 0-15-205683-1

First edition
H G F E D C B A

The illustrations in this book were done in pen-and-ink and watercolors.
The display type and text type were set in P22 Garamouche.
Color separations by Bright Arts Ltd., Hong Kong
Manufactured by South China Printing Company, Ltd., China
This book was printed on totally chlorine-free Enso Stora Matte paper.
Production supervision by Ginger Boyer
Designed by Linda Lockowitz

For Elizabeth Harding—surprise!
—L. N.

For my wife, Victoria
—V. G.

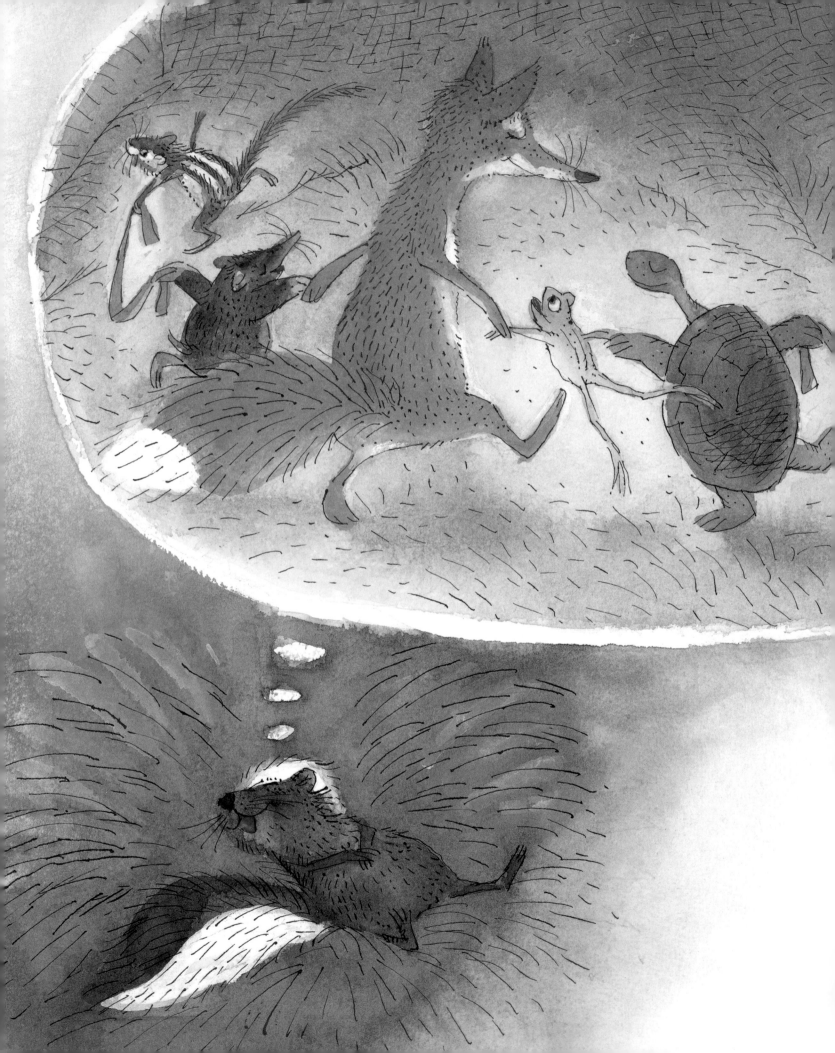

The very day that winter ends,
Skunk wakes from dreaming of her friends.

She blinks her eyes and shakes her head,
then jumps right up and makes her bed.

"Hooray! My winter nap is done!
It's time for me to have some fun."

Skunk yawns and stretches, twists and bends,
then scurries off to find her friends.

"Good morning, Turtle," calls out Skunk.
"Where are you, Mole? Hello, Chipmunk."

Skunk listens hard and smells the air,
but does not find them anywhere.

"Where are my friends? Where can they be?
Have all of them forgotten me?"

"Perhaps they hate the way I smell."
Skunk stamps her feet and starts to yell.

But no one hears Skunk rant and rave.
(Not even Bear inside his cave.)

Skunk is thirsty, sad, and hot.
"A drink," she says, "would hit the spot."

She sighs and gives herself a shake,
then slowly trudges to the lake.

Skunk's friends are waiting on the sand
to welcome Skunk as they had planned.
Bunny hops about. "Oh dear,
I thought by now Skunk would be here."

"She always wakes and takes a drink."
Fox sniffs and says, "That's her, I think."
"Hush," says Turtle, with a wink.
"Don't scare her or she'll make a stink."

"Skunk!" squeals Mole. "How do you do?
We've got a big surprise for you.
For months we've planned a talent show.
Ready or not, Skunk, here we go!"

Fox shows Skunk Frog's favorite joke.
Frog laughs so hard he starts to croak.

Turtle strikes a Skunk-like pose,
then dances lightly on his toes.

Chipmunk tosses nuts and sticks,
and teaches Skunk some juggling tricks.

Mole dances like an acrobat,
while Crow flips Bunny from a hat.

Snake and Ladybug hum a note,
then sing a song for Skunk they wrote.

Ant swings Beetle by the knees,
then lands in front of Skunk with ease.

"The end," say Beetle, Ant, and Crow.
"We hope that you enjoyed the show!"

"That's not the end." Skunk starts to rise.
"I also have a spring surprise."

Skunk leaps up to take the stage.
She reads the words upon her page.

"When I wake from my winter's sleep,
I love to hear the robins peep.
I love to smell the sweet spring breeze.
I love to see the budding trees."

"When I wake from my winter's rest,
I'll tell you what I love the best:
To see my friends down by the lake
makes me so glad to be awake."

Skunk's friends all clap and make a fuss.
"We love the poem you wrote for us."

"And we love YOU," her friends all sing.
They hug and kiss her. "Happy spring!"